Dear Parent:

Congratulations! Your child is taking the first steps on an exciting journey. The destination? Independent reading!

STEP INTO READING® will help your child get there. The program offers books at five levels that accompany children from their first attempts at reading to reading success. Each step includes fun stories, fiction and nonfiction, and colorful art. There are also Step into Reading Sticker Books, Step into Reading Math Readers, and Step into Reading Phonics Readers—a complete literacy program with something to interest every child.

Learning to Read, Step by Step!

Ready to Read Preschool–Kindergarten
- **big type and easy words • rhyme and rhythm • picture clues**

For children who know the alphabet and are eager to begin reading.

Reading with Help Preschool–Grade 1
- **basic vocabulary • short sentences • simple stories**

For children who recognize familiar words and sound out new words with help.

Reading on Your Own Grades 1–3
- **engaging characters • easy-to-follow plots • popular topics**

For children who are ready to read on their own.

Reading Paragraphs Grades 2–3
- **challenging vocabulary • short paragraphs • exciting stories**

For newly independent readers who read simple sentences with confidence.

Ready for Chapters Grades 2–4
- **chapters • longer paragraphs • full-color art**

For children who want to take the plunge into chapter books but still like colorful pictures.

STEP INTO READING® is designed to give every child a successful reading experience. The grade levels are only guides. Children can progress through the steps at their own speed, developing confidence in their reading, no matter what their grade.

Remember, a lifetime love of reading starts with a single step!

To my favorite poodle, Goodness VanSchuyver
—J.S.

For Rusty, and all good dogs
—P.M.

 Published in the United States by Random House Children's Books, a division of Random House, Inc., New York, and simultaneously in Canada by Random House of Canada Limited, Toronto.

www.stepintoreading.com

Educators and librarians, for a variety of teaching tools, visit us at
www.randomhouse.com/teachers

Library of Congress Cataloging-in-Publication Data
Sierra, Judy.
Coco and Cavendish : circus dogs / by Judy Sierra ; illustrated by Paul Meisel.
p. cm. — (Step into reading. A step 3 book)
SUMMARY: When the owner of the circus where they work replaces them with robot dogs, Coco and Cavendish set out to find a new job—but it is not as easy as they thought it would be.
ISBN 0-375-82237-2 (trade) — ISBN 0-375-92237-7 (lib. bdg.)
[1. Poodles—Fiction. 2. Border collie—Fiction. 3. Dogs—Fiction. 4. Circus—Fiction.]
I. Meisel, Paul, ill. II. Title. III. Series: Step into reading. Step 3 book.
PZ7.S5773 Co 2003 [E]—dc21 2002013096

Printed in the United States of America First Edition 10 9 8 7 6 5 4 3 2 1

STEP INTO READING® STEP 3

Coco and Cavendish
Circus Dogs

by Judy Sierra
illustrated by Paul Meisel

Random House New York

Chapter 1

Circus Dogs

My name is Coco.

I am a poodle.

My best friend is Cavendish.

He's a border collie.

We are wonderful.

We can't help it.

We are dogs.

Once upon a time,

Cavendish and I were the stars

of the Zazzlehoff Circus.

We wore diamond collars.

We ate T-bone steaks.

I walked on the high wire.

Cavendish played Frisbee.

We sang. We danced.

We pulled down the clown's pants.

The crowd went bananas.

Our best trick was House-on-Fire.
“Help! Fire! Save my baby!”
yelled the mama clown.
The house was fake,
the fire was fake,
and the baby was really
a grown-up clown.

Cavendish ran up the ladder
and saved the clown baby.
I held the hose in my mouth
and sprayed water on the fire.
The crowd went bonkers.

Zelda was the boss
of the Zazzlehoff Circus.

One cold morning,

she gave us a pink slip of paper:

Dear Cavendish and Coco,

You are fired.

Love,

Zelda

"I don't feel TIRED," said Cavendish.

"No, you dippy dog," said Zelda.

"You are FIRED.

Meet the new stars

of the Zazzlehoff Circus."

Two dogs whirred into the ring.

They were not real dogs.

They were robots.

“Torbo and Orbot can do your tricks,”
Zelda said,
“and they don’t eat T-bone steaks.”
“They don’t make puddles, either,”
said the fake baby clown.
“We don’t make puddles!”
I yipped.

Zelda put our collars
on Torbo and Orbot.
The robots wagged their fake tails—
CLANG, CLANG, CLANG.
"Let's get out of here,"
growled Cavendish.

Chapter 2

Hunting Dogs

"What are we going to do, Coco?"
asked Cavendish sadly.
"We will get jobs,"
I told Cavendish.
"We had jobs at the circus.
There must be more jobs for dogs."

We walked and walked.

I saw a sign

in a window:

WAITERS WANTED

Cavendish and I went inside.

We sat on the floor.

We did not move.

We waited and waited.

A man in a white hat saw us.
"No dogs allowed!" he yelled.
He chased us out the door.

We walked and walked
until we saw another sign:
SITTERS WANTED
"Sitting is easy,"
yipped Cavendish.

BABYSITTERS
INC.

We went inside and we sat
and sat and sat.
A lady in a red dress saw us.
"Oh! Dog germs!" she yelled.
She chased us out the door.

Chapter 3
Junkyard Dogs

"Don't worry,"

I told Cavendish.

"We will find good jobs."

I tried to wag my tail.

My tail would not wag.

It was too sad.

Then we saw the best sign yet:
WATCHDOGS WANTED
"We will be good watchdogs,"
I barked.

"Yes," Cavendish yipped.

"At the Zazzlehoff Circus,

everyone watched us."

The junk man smiled at us.

We sang and we danced.

We played junkyard Frisbee.

The junk man laughed.
"You dogs are smart," he said.
"But I need mean dogs."
"Grrr," growled Cavendish.
I tried to look mean, too,
but that is hard for a poodle.
"You are too nice to be watchdogs,"
the junk man said.
"But it's cold tonight.
Why don't you sleep here?"

The man gave us a bowl of dog food.

We lay down on an old sofa.

I dreamed about my warm bed

at the Zazzlehoff Circus.

But not for long.

Chapter 4
Hero Dogs

I felt a nip on my ear.

"Wake up, Coco! I smell smoke,"
yelped Cavendish.

I opened my eyes.

I heard a shout.

"Help! Fire! Save my baby!"

We ran to the gate.

But it was locked.

Cavendish took a running start

and jumped up, up, and over the gate!

Then we dug a tunnel,

Cavendish from his side,

and me from my side.

And I ran out of the junkyard.

We followed our noses
to a burning building.

A little girl was shouting,
"Save my baby kitten!"

The kitten was on a high ledge.
"Cavendish!" I barked.
"Can you jump up
to the fire escape?"
Cavendish took his biggest jump
up, up, and onto the fire escape.

"Come here!" Cavendish barked
to the kitten.
The kitten did not move.
"Please come here," he begged.
The kitten hissed.
"This kitten is not as smart
as the clown baby,"
Cavendish growled.

"Think, Cavendish," I barked.

"How does the mother tiger carry
her cubs at the circus?"
Cavendish picked up the kitten
in his mouth
and carried her to the little girl.

Chapter 5
Fire Dogs

"Smile for the camera,"
the TV reporter told us.
Cavendish and I smiled and smiled.
"Tonight at the Hunter Hotel
these stray dogs saved a kitten's life,"
said the TV reporter.
The fire chief rubbed us behind the ears.
"You are so smart and brave," he said.
"You would be great fire dogs."

TV
NEWS

I smelled a familiar smell.

It was Zelda.

"These are not stray dogs!"

she yelled at the TV reporter.

"They belong to me."

Zelda put leashes on Cavendish and me.
"Now that you are TV stars,
people will pay lots of money
to see you," she told us.
"You are coming back to the circus."

The next day, we did our old tricks.
But we did them in a new way.
Cavendish played Frisbee with Zelda's wig.

I gave the clown baby a bath.

The crowd went berserk.

Torbo and Orbot had new jobs
cleaning up after the elephants.
They growled at us,
RRRR, RRRR, RRRR.
"Be quiet," I barked.

“You metal mutts
can be the stars
of the Zazzlehoff Circus.
We are getting better jobs.”

"We should be fire dogs,"

I told Cavendish.

"We are smart and we are brave.

The fire chief said so."

"Uh-oh," barked Cavendish.

"Here comes Zelda to fire us again."

"Let's get out of here," I barked.

Cavendish and I ran away
from the Zazzlehoff Circus.
We followed our noses
to the fire station.
We would be fire dogs at last!